OLD JOE

JoAnn Nyman

JoAnn Nyman

Old Joe

JoAnn Nyman

ACKNOWLEDGEMENTS

Thanks to My Sweetheart John, who never once complained about the hours I've spent on this project.

CONTENTS

JoAnn Nyman

OLD JOE

This is a story about Old Joe.

Now Old Joe wasn't all that old. He was aged enough to have a few grey hairs, a couple of scars and a bunch of stories to tell, some were true some were not so true. He knew a little bit about a lot of folks. Most people that knew him didn't have too much bad to say on his behalf.

He tried to be fair and honest in his dealings. Once, "A man of true integrity," was said about him and he was highly embarrassed.

Joe was generally good natured although he did get riled up when others weren't pulling their share of the load or when they left him to pick up their slack because of their inability to see a job through to the end.

Anyone, who knew Joe, knew if he was displeased with something by the clenched lips and the tongue working the inside of his cheek.

Joe knew a few cus words, but he rarely advertised them.

He enjoyed a friendly game of penny poker and had won more than one fair sized pot on a possible full house. He always said that was his "Lucky Hand".

He tried to be the kind of man that could anticipate where he was needed before being told and he lacked patience with the ranch hand that had no common sense or ambition to be a self-starter.

Joe wasn't a tall man, mostly average in height and weight, sandy blond hair in his younger days, dull and greyish in his later years. His locks curled when they needed a trim or when they were soaked with sweat.

Joe sported a respectable mustache; in fact, many were quite envious of it.

His blue eyes were clear and bright, not like some of the ranch hands that burned the candle at both ends or those who watered down the awake hours with too much whiskey. Joe took a nip now and again, but he knew when to quit.

Joe stood erect and walked with purpose. He sat upright, never slouching or sprawling.

Old Joe

When it was time to relax, he laid right out and went to sleep. It was mostly easy for Joe to get a good night's rest, as he had a clear conscious, never felt like he had to be watching his back. He was trustworthy and trusted others until they gave him reason not to.

He judged others by their actions, not by what they "said" they "had done" or were "gonna do" someday.

You would never notice Joe standing in a crowd by his looks alone, but judge him by his common sense, the devotion he had to his friends or his integrity and values, and Old Joe was in a class by himself.

Joe didn't lay claim to a wife or sweetheart, so after the work was done in the fall, the majority of the men on the ranch would take their pay and go back home while Joe stuck around and tended to the cattle throughout the winter.

Every evening after grub, Joe and the other ranch hands would sit around the campfire, tell jokes and stories, tease each other, discuss the events of the day and plan the course of action for the next day.

As the fire burned down to a soft red glow and the stomping of horse hooves grew scarce, Virgil the camp jack and his helper would clean up the mess from the evening meal and get things prepared for morning.

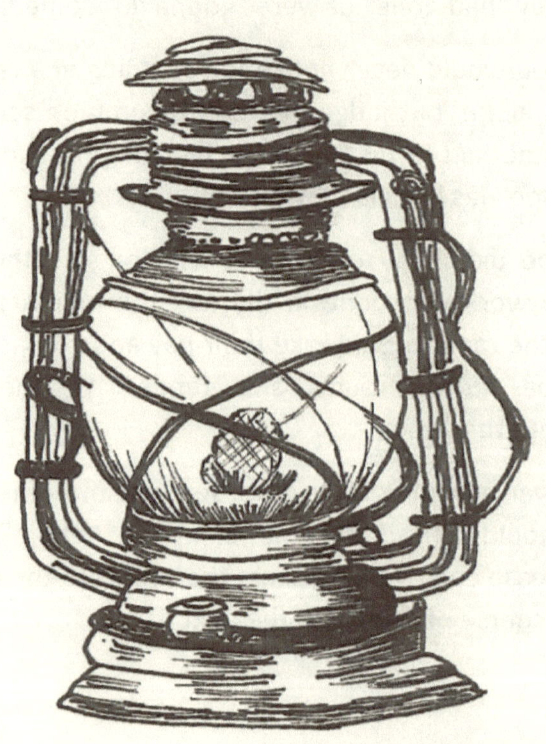

Old Joe

Slowly one by one, the hands would slink off to their bedrolls. All except one, Old Joe.

Night after night, as regular as a twenty-dollar pocket watch, Old Joe would quietly slip away behind the chuck wagon. He would turn the lantern light down low and hang it on an old rusty nail near the toolbox. On a wooden bench, Joe would sit and write in a well-worn, store-bought book line upon line, ever so neatly.

Sometimes he wrote fast and furious, sometimes slow and deliberate contemplating every word before putting it down, pausing and staring as if searching for a thought or listening for a far-off distant howl of a lonely coyote. Then, one more line or two and Joe would pocket his pencil and read over his words.

Coming to the end, he would take out his old timer. Methodically he would score the page and then proceed to tear it out of the book.

Old Joe took great care to fold the page perfectly, first in half then in thirds. He would snuff out the lantern and return it to its proper hook in the wagon.

With deliberation and resolve, Joe would then walk directly to the dying embers, stop, look at the manuscript, back at the firepit, then bend over carefully placing the folded document in the hottest spot still glowing.

Joe waited patiently as the paper ignited and became engulfed in a rekindled flame. He would stand staring at the fire before closing his eyes and bowing his head, sometimes for a few seconds, sometimes for several minutes.

No-one ever asked what he was doing although everyone in camp was aware of the nightly ritual. Occasionally they would look at one another with raised eyebrow and shrug, or elbow each other and nod, but no one quizzed Old Joe nor even spoke out loud about the peculiar evening happenings.

JOSIE'S PRESENTS HER INQUIRY

Day after day I had wondered without taking action, but tonight my curiosity was more than I could control. Twice I arose and took a step towards Joe and the wagon to inquire of his strange habit. Twice I caught myself and retreated to safety. On the third attempt I didn't slow down. I was determined.

The length of the trip to Old Joe and the Chuck Wagon was no longer than a lariat but it seemed like miles. I could feel the others gasp in disbelief as all eyes and ears in camp followed my every move.

I tipped up a log laying on its side as a makeshift seat and as casually as possible, sat down next to Joe.

He looked up gawking at me with puzzlement as though he had never met me since Adam. Without breaking our eye contact, he leisurely closed his journal and replaced his pencil into his pocket.

He eyed me up and down. I felt mortified at myself for barging in on his personal space.

Seconds seemed like forever and a day, then he smiled a little crooked Mona Lisa smile and asked, "Can I help you with something?"

I froze in silence, surprised that he spoke and embarrassed at my lack of preparation. I had no idea what to say.

"Did you need something?" He repeated. "Well Josie, can I help you?"

"I, uh, um, well ya see," I stammered, "I was um, uh wondering what you um, uh are doing?

Old Joe

Joe's smile spread across his face. He snickered, "Well, why don't ya ask me if you want to know?"

Having no comeback ready, I felt like a kid standing behind a shed in front of their Dad armed with a freshly cut willow. I shrugged my shoulders clear up to my ears and stuttered, "I a-a-am asking."

I must have looked mighty silly 'cause Joe laughed out loud a warm, friendly, inviting laugh.

His hand reached out to my shoulder and we both hooted like two young hyenas' .

"I'll tell you what," he spoke as the laughter faded, "you come back tomorrow night when it's not so late, and I'll tell you a story."

I nodded, stretched out my hand for a shake and mumbled, "You're on Pard, talk to you tomorrow."

Self-conscious about my casual choice of words, I arose and headed for bed.

The trip back across camp didn't seem nearly as long.

I looked back at Old Joe; in his hand I could see what appeared to be a deck of cards. On second glance, I realized it was his bandana folded neatly just the size of the palm of your hand. Joe looked at it and gradually drew it near his face. He patted first one eye then the other then quickly tucked it back into his vest pocket.

I became aware of the quiet murmur around me as I untied my bed roll, yet no one spoke directly to me. I had no idea until that moment that the whole camp had been watching me bravely confront Joe.

Old Joe returned to his book and sat motionless for quite a few minutes. Eventually he preceded as usual, finished the page, then added another and surprisingly yet another.

The night was especially quiet as he neared the fire ring. All the whispers ceased giving way to the crickets, whoot owls and the comforting gentle night noises.

Tonight's ritual was just like every other night only more animated, more deliberate and the pause as he bowed his head seemed to last an eternity.

Old Joe

Eventually Joe sauntered leisurely back to his bed roll. I noticed as always, his bed was positioned halfway between the older fully-grown cow hands assembly and the little group of us subordinate younger hands.

It was several minutes before sleep was allowed to set in as I pondered what information was instore for me on the morrow.

JoAnn Nyman

THE NEXT DAY; KATIE

Joe was up before the rest of the camp and out observing over the herd. He took note of the starlit sky, walked through the rope pen of the remuda looking for anything that might be amiss. He found his grey and slipped her a sugar cube as he fondly stroked her muzzle.

When he returned to camp Joe saw that as usual, Katie was already up. As Virg's right-hand man so to speak, she was stoking up the fire so the logs could burn down into hot embers for cooking breakfast.

Katie was a natural born chef and when given the chance never ceased to impress Virgil or the others eager to try out her culinary skills.

Katie had already updated and checked the ledger book she was in charge of. It was actually Virgil's responsibility to keep daily tab on work and inventory, but Virg's penmanship and spelling were less than desirable. Katie, on the other hand, penned like a monk hand printing a bible cover page, her spelling was flawless, and her calculations were always spot on.

In no way did Virg's shortcomings in record keeping reflect his skill in syphering, cattle management or general intelligence. He may have been a little long in the tooth, a bit crotchety, short tempered and demanding, but he was well respected by all the hands at the JR Bar ranch, especially Katie.

Virg was a big man. His twisted fingers, grey hair, round belly and bowed legs testified of years of hard work.

Katie had the sour dough set up for pancakes. Finding that she had a few minutes before the crew awoke, Katie positioned herself near the lit lantern to finish mending a shirt for another young hand on the ranch, Billy Joe, who had somehow snagged a sleeve on a tree branch.

As she darned, Katie wondered why all the men including Virgil and Old Joe insisted on calling him just plain "Billy" despite his preference to being called "Billy Joe."

She reasoned that men just like to get a raise out of each other, although it never caused irritation to Billy Joe as he always saw the good in others and discounted the negative.

She autographed the patch in the same manor that she marked all the patches she sewed, with a tiny embroidered daisy, her personal brand. It was hardly big enough to notice, but she knew it was there and kissed it for luck.

Katie smiled to herself the same smile she shared with everyone, a smile that could warm the heart of the devil and make him want to do good.

Sounding like a songbird, softly singing a hymn of praise to the Lord, Katie gathered her sewing supplies and placed them into a satchel with a pile of wildlife and landscape drawings and paintings. She had run out of her favorite colors of paint and the half-finished works waited for her patiently until she could find someone going to town to replenish her supplies.

Katie added a few more logs to the fire and turned off the oil to the lamp. It was getting lighter now as the early morning dawn filtered itself through the trees. Joe watched from a short way off and blinked away a drop of emotion building up within his heart.

Matt appeared around the chuck wagon carrying a spare bridle and placed it in the supply wagon. In his hand was a small tin cup filled to the brim with freshly picked wild raspberries and a small bouquet of wildflowers. Two things he knew that Katie loved.

He walked to the back of the chuck wagon and set them nonchalantly on the folded-down side panel of the wagon where Katie would eventually find them.

Matt had assigned himself the daily task of inspecting the company tack and keeping it in good repair. He personally made sure that the ranch's canvas tents, lean-tos and wagon covers in a wet bedroll were kept hole-free and in tip-top condition.

Matt hated sleeping in a a wet bed and assumed everyone else did as well. When time permitted, he mended, dressed up the utility bridles and such with beautiful leather tooling or braided rawhide edges just for good looks.

He and Katie were close. Billy Joe and J.J. kept a watch out for Katie and Josie, but not nearly as much as Matt who seemed a bit more interested in Katie than necessary. Nobody appeared to notice, all but Joe that is. He always perceived small nuances in all the young hands.

It was coming daybreak. Josie was up now, braiding her long silky auburn hair into a thick rope to keep it out of the way as she would be working with the colts today.

As she was waiting for the coffee to boil, Virgil grinned at her and went back to laying out bacon strips on the grill to fry. Josie thought he might ask about her talk with Old Joe from the previous night, but she was relieved when he didn't.

Josie tried to focus on her upcoming responsibilities with the young horses for today. She wanted to please Old Joe and earn her keep. Josie didn't realize that her expertise with horses was admired by every member of the camp and she had already earned more than their respect. Her courage in climbing on a rank animal was a well-known fact among the hands.

Figuring she had a few minutes before breakfast was ready and deciding that Katie and Virg had mealtime under control, Josie slipped away into the thick cover of vegetation.

Under concealment, she knelt to have a talk with the Lord. Her simple words flowed like poetry as she acknowledged the blessings bestowed upon her and the individuals she worked with, requested the Lords guidance and asked for a guardian angel to be present over their little company.

When Josie felt she had adequately expressed her gratitude, she quoted a line from Psalms and said her Amen.

Returning to camp, Josie slipped over next to Virg and Katie and began to pull out the tin cups, plates and utensils that would be needed for their morning meal.

As each hand in the outfit arose, they suspiciously eyed Josie. Some watched her every move, some tipped their hats courteously, others paused as they passed by wanting to speak. None were forward enough to do so.

Old Joe

It didn't take long for all the crew, young and old, to get moving once Virgil clamored on that blasted triangle shaped chow bell. And within minutes everyone's belly was full, and their horses saddled ready to go. There was a day of work ahead of them and everyone knew their part.

JoAnn Nyman

MATT'S GRAND ADVENTURE

It was mid-morning when Joe came upon Matt again. He stopped to see what the lad was up to. It didn't take him long to discern what had happened.

Matt was riding a young buckskin filly that day and her inexperience had caused the two of them to be in a perfect position for an interesting predicament, or better known and referred to as a "Grand Adventure" by Matt.

While inching down a dry rocky incline, Matt and the young filly had come across a rattlesnake sunning itself on the rocks. Unaccustomed to having a rider on her back, the buckskin did what her instincts told her to do, and that was to jump sideways to clear any possible chance of an attack from the diamond backed enemy.

In doing so, Matt was unseated and ended up a foot while the youngster ran off a short distance and stood shaking and snorting. Still upset by the snake, the filly nervously moved farther and farther away from Matt every time he made an attempt to catch her.

Joe watched unobserved and impressed with the tolerance Matt exhibited. Matt's green eyes never left the filly. He stopped moving and allowed her to settle. He watched and talked to his charge with the patience of Job.

"That was Matt for you," thought Joe, "patient, patient, patient... right up to the point when he wasn't, then you better look out."

Old Joe chuckled to himself. He had seen Matt come unglued only once or twice, just like someone else Joe had known and had been in his life a long time ago. He shook off the thought of the past.

Confident that Matt and his tender way with animals would prevail with the filly, Joe turned "Blue Lass" his grey mare silently around and returned to the herd and the rest of the crew.

J.J.

Around noon Joe realized he hadn't seen J.J. for rather some time. He glanced around at all the riders looking for J.J.'s signature green paisley bandana. It was quite possibly the largest and greenest bandana in the state. J.J. was never without it, said it gave him "good luck".

Joe knew J.J. was assigned to be patrolling the southern section of their grazing land making sure the cattle didn't wander too near the quicksand springs or get on the wrong side of the washed-out gully.

Joe turned his mount towards the south. It was his job to keep track of the young hands, whether they needed supervision or not. J.J. could always be counted on to fulfill his duties. But more so, J.J. and his infectious sense of humor could be counted on to make things around camp fun and entertaining. He was the first one in camp to pull a joke on some other hand or more often tell an amusing anecdote on himself.

One-week J.J. started out by putting a very small pebble in the right toe of Matt and Billy Joe's boots. It took a couple of hours before they both had to shuck their boot and remove it.

The next day J.J. placed a little bit bigger stone in each boot. Again, both boys had to stop, remove their boots to shake out the pebble in order to continue the day.

On day three, Matt and Billy Joe, wise to the pebble trick, shook out their boots, quickly pulled them on in the early morning dark and went to work figuring they had outsmarted their jokester. What they didn't realize was that J.J. had switched their boots out with each other.

It took half a day for them to realize they were wearing each other's boots. By then Matt's toes were cramping up and Billy Joe's boots had all but fallen off his feet three times.

No one ever outright accused J.J. of his mischief, and he never readily admitted his part in the boot incident. But when Billy Joe was sharing the story at the nightly campfire, J.J.'s twinkle in his eye and his deepening dimples from trying to hide a smile, gave him away to Joe.

Thinking about that trick, Joe snickered to himself.

Old Joe

Nearing where J.J. was expected to be, Joe saw J.J.'s sorrel in the shade, tied to a fallen log. Joe knew J.J. must be close by. Sure enough, about 20 yards up the side hill J.J. could be seen picking chokecherries and placing them carefully into his green bandana to take back to Virg. He knew that with a couple pounds of sugar and those berries, Virgil could make a batch of jelly for the crew.

Joe's mouth watered. There was nothing better than Katie's biscuits, her fresh churned butter and Virg's chokecherry jelly. Joe reminisced back to a warm summers' day when he had spent a passionate afternoon and evening on a blanket, near a creek, sharing just such a treat with someone special. His chin quivered as he worked the inside of his right cheek with his tongue than slowly wiped his cheek with the back of his hand.

Joe wasn't interested in reprimanding J.J. for not being on task. He knew J.J. had checked his area and would be back in place as soon as possible, and besides the crew would all benefit from his hike up the hill.

JoAnn Nyman

BILLY JOE

Joe dismounted and tightened his cinch, checked the mare's hooves and saddled up heading back north to where Billy Joe was checking out the possibility of moving the cattle down to the lower country through a questionable canyon.

It was quite a while before Joe reached the rim of the canyon.

"Billy Joe should be meandering down through the bottom," he thought. "checking for dangerous sections along the trail."

Joe stopped on the edge of an outcrop of granite rock and scanned the canyon. The leaves on all the trees were dry and dusty. Autumns first frost was still a few weeks off. Later in the year Joe would be able to see the canyon floor but not until the maples and aspens had shed their red and golden foliage.

Joe sat for several minutes watching when he heard a strange noise. He wasn't sure exactly what it was at first, but assumed it was Billy Joe or possibly an elk stumbling through the brush. The noise seemed to be coming from down the canyon.

Skirting along the rock-strewn rim, Joe eased Blue Lass into a better position to be able to see where the noise was coming from.

Joe was just about to holler out, when he came into view of Billy Joe. It initially looked as if Billy Joe was in distress laying over a large log, arms outstretched, his bay gelding standing off in the distance. Upon further examination, Joe could see that Billy Joe was struggling with something intertwined in the thick downfall.

Old Joe

Joe stopped to evaluate the situation, just as a lowly distressed bawl erupted from behind the log. It became apparent that a young calf had gotten itself in quite a predicament and had a hind leg twisted and caught between several large branches of a fallen red pine.

Billy Joe was holding the panic-stricken calf down trying to get it to relax long enough to be able to reposition the leg to where it could be removed from the rubble.

The calf's mother stood not more than 10 yards away, head down, ready to attack anything and anyone who dared cause harm to her calf. She stomped and pawed at the ground like a Mexican Fighting Bull.

Billy Joe was well aware of her presence behind him. She was a big nasty tempered thing and could easily do a man damage or worse. He knew his own safety was in jeopardy. He also knew that his chance of getting out of this situation depended upon getting that calf released from its trap and headed back to the old cow.

There was nothing Joe could do to help as he was more than 200 yards away and there was no trail or open route to where Billy Joe and the calf were.

It would take Joe 20 minutes or more to backtrack and make his way to the bottom of the canyon on the best of horses. The circumstances would be substantially different by the time he arrived to help. All Joe could do was watch and pray.

Billy Joe's face was red with the effort he was exerting. Sweat mixed with the dust in the air from the struggling of the calf covered the prominent freckles Billy so conspicuously wore.

There was no hint of little boy in his appearance today. At this moment Billy Joe was a man doing a man's job.

Old Joe stood motionless, fist clenched and jaw tight. He knew this scenario could go either way.

"That's no newborn." he thought to himself.

It was an early spring calf and easily quadrupled Billy Joe's weight. Tougher then nails that kid was, but his physical growing hadn't caught up to his age yet and most folks would describe him as a little on the scrawny side.

Billy Joe was winded and exhausted, but he never backed off. He made his way to the calf's head, rotated it back across its shoulder and covered its eyes. Speaking in a calm and reassuring voice he repeated, "Easy there, easy ...easy... easy"

The peaceful voice and calm hands did the trick. Soon the calf began to respond to the tranquil sound. Even the old bally cow began to relax and stood just watching and waiting.

With his right hand still on the calf's head, quickly and proficiently Billy Joe slid his left hand across the calf's back and down its hip, finally coming to its hock, where he skillfully in one swift motion, maneuvered the appendage out of its snare. In a split second the calf was up and set on a coarse straight to its mother, staggering some, but with no permanent damage done.

Billy Joe noticed the oddly shaped white spot on the calf's right rib. He remembered that spotted calf. It was a breach birth, first one Billy had to pull by himself.

"Funny about coincidences." he thought, "or maybe that darn calf is just plain "lucky".

Billy Joe's next thought was that he was happy to not have to put the calf down with a broken leg. He always hated having to report bad news to Joe even if it did mean fresh beef for supper. Although he wouldn't admit it, Billy hated to see any animal in pain or have to be shot.

Taking a deep breath, Billy Joe brushed off the broken twigs, leaves and dirt then he sat down on the large log to take inventory. A few bruises, cuts and scrapes were all he had to contend with.

He shook his head with a smile at a riddled sleeve, a ripped shirt pocket and a hole in his britches. He would have to really sweeten up Katie before requesting "this" major patch job.

Old Joe thankful and relieved at the outcome of events, shouted out to Billy, "You OK?"

Billy looked up, still shaken a bit, cheerfully answered, "All is well, just another chore."

They both knew differently.

With a wave of his hat, Joe moved off, leaving Billy with time to contemplate and collected himself.

Billy looked around to evaluate the trail leading down the canyon. He would have to find a better direction to lead the cattle into the low land.

While gazing around at the options before him, Billy noticed the spectacular landscape around him and an immense variety of wildflowers. Prominent in the area were his favorites, purple and lavender columbine.

Billy tested his memory by silently reciting their names to himself. He reached down and picked up a stone from the ground. A smooth stone, it was red zebra jasper, shaped like a heart.

Billy looked around and up to the heavens. He inaudibly thanked God for the health of the calf, his own safety, the beauty around him and the banded sign of remembrance he had come across.

Billy Joe was sure this stunning stone was a gift from his from his guardian angel.

Billy sat for a few minutes until his impatient pony nickered softly and caught his attention. Unaware of the seriousness of the preceding trials, his tethered mount had grown tired of waiting and was anxious to be on their way.

Billy became aware of his own thirst and hunger. He wished he was nearer to where J.J. was working that day. Billy knew that J.J. always had a piece of jerky or a left-over biscuit rolled up, unnoticeably hidden in the folds of that silly green bandana.

The beautiful striped nugget, one more "Good Luck Charm" collected from nature, found its way into Billy's pocket as he ambled to his gelding, mounted and went back to work.

JOSIE RECOUNTS HER DAY

The day drug on and on, my mind wandered off time after time in anticipation of nightfall and the mysterious story that Old Joe was about to revealed.

Finally, dusk arrived; I was glad not to have to worry about night watch, someone else could handle the babysitting, besides I had something else concerning my thoughts.

Virg's rabbit stew was barely swallowed, and Katie was hurriedly cleaning up supper plates when J.J. stretched.

"Think I'll call it a day." He yawned.

Billy Joe followed within minutes, "I'm a bit achy tonight, maybe a little shut eye would help."

Matt stood and paced back and forth a time or two then without a word ambled off into the dark

The race to bed was on. The obvious descend from the campfire was noticeably awkward. Within minutes Joe and I were all alone at the campfire.

Old Joe rolled his eyes and poked in the fire with a willow stick for a while, as I watched the sun pull the last shadows of the day across the tops of the mountains and down the other side.

Eventually Joe arose and meandered to his usual sitting place, lit the lantern and pulled out the brown dog-eared book.

I wanted to jump up and skip over to where he sat. I was so eager to learn of his undisclosed story. It was a chore to constrain myself a good respectable amount of time before I proceeded in his direction.

As I approached Joe looked up. He leaned over and propped up my makeshift chair from the previous evening.

I sat slowly and remained quiet as a church mouse. Joe went back to his book, finished a line then stopped.

I opened my mouth to speak but his pointer finger waving in the air, caused me to immediately freeze. Joe's hand held me at bay in sort of a threatening way.

Ten, twenty, thirty seconds ticked by, but it seemed like half a lifetime. At that point, just as sharply as he had raised it, his hand fell to his lap. Joe scribbled the end of a thought, then closed his binder.

"Guess I've caused quite a stir 'round here." He said. "Didn't know everybody was so concerned with what I do."

He chuckled, "Don't know whether to be embarrassed, pissed off or flattered."

I listened intently; eyes fixated on the top of my boots. I thought it might be too uncomfortable for Joe if I looked right at him. But actually, I guess it was me who was uncomfortable.

"Well Josie" he said, "I guess I made a promise to you, let's get on with it." Joe took a big deep breath and let it out slowly. He brought his hand up to his chin and stroked his bristly whiskers between his thumb and index finger.

"I ain't telling this but one time start to finish, so you better gather "um up."

I wasn't sure what he meant so I just sat looking at him with a blank expression on my face. While I tried to figure it out. Joe motioned with a swipe of his hand to "get up".

I stood up still bewildered and He repeated, "Gather 'um up girl, go get the rest, everybody's 'gonna hear this from me, one time start to finish, so you all get the story straight."

Expecting them to all be in their bed rolls, I turned and set off to gather Katie and the boys. To my surprise, halfway there I ran right into them darn busybodies face to face.

They had been lurking off in the distance just past the reach of the lantern light in an attempt to eavesdrop. We bumped into each other like a blind calf looking for its mother in a snowstorm.

Righting ourselves we tried to regain our composure and walked back to Joe who was seated back at the campfire. Standing there in a row like little toy soldiers Joe looked at us.

Joe stood, rolled his eyes and shook his head. "Stoke up the fire and pull up a seat. I'll be back in a minute. I've got to go get something."

We all grabbed some downfall and gathered around the campfire.

THE CAMPFIRE

Word had gotten around to the older hands about the upcoming explanation to Josie. When they saw Josie invite the young hands to join in the presentation, the adult men casually wandered from their own camp area to the smaller campfire Joe's little cowboys utilized.

The seasoned hands knew they were treading on ground that was not theirs to tread upon.

They expected the young'uns to keep clear of the main camp, and respectfully they kept out of the kid's area.

But tonight was different as the men, including Virgil and Wilf, the ranch boss, humbly entered unknown territory and respectfully took up second row seating behind Katie, Josie, Matt, Billy Joe and J.J.

When Joe returned, he was visibly dismayed at the sight of all those eager faces. In his hands a reddish-brown cedar box made a conspicuous appearance. Joe placed the box on the ground to the side and around back behind the stump he claimed as a seat.

He was embarrassed and self-conscious. He considered backing out of his promise to Josie, but he knew he would have to answer her request at some time or another. It might as well be now, although this is not how he envisioned reciting his story.

He picked up a large cedar log and gingerly placed it in the center of the burning firewood, then sat down on a strategically placed stump.

Old Joe

Rubbing the side of his cheek with the palm of his hand, Joe gazed deeply into the fire as though searching for a lost thought.

He took an exaggerated deep breath and let it out very slowly, followed by two more of the same.

Looking around at the five young eager faces as well as the seasoned hands, Joe smiled...

JoAnn Nyman

JOE'S STORY

Without prompting or any further ado, Joe took one last deep laborious breath, letting it out slowly he began.

"I never knew my parents. Rumor has it that they were killed in an Indian raid but I ain't never believed that. Nevertheless, I spent my childhood (if that's what you want ta' call it) in an orphanage.

"It wasn't much of a place to grow up. Mostly the crotchety old couple that ran the place kept us fed and gave us a bed with one blanket in the summer and two in the winter if we done our chores and behaved.

"As soon as any of us kids were old enough to be of any help to anyone, we'd be 'loaned out' as hired hands. I took my turn, starting when I was about eight, feeding sows on a pig ranch all one hot and miserable summer.

"I was thankful in the fall when they slaughtered most of the pigs to hang in the smoke house for winter meat. That ended that occupation, and I was drug back into the abusive hands of the bad-tempered couple.

"My next failed occupation was helping a poor dirt farmer ready his ground for a crop of corn. We worked that ground north and south then east and west then north and south again until it was clean and soft for planting those seeds.

"We planted those seeds three in a hole 10-inches apart clear across that 20 acres. I thought all we were gonna have to do next was watch them plants grow, but hell was I wrong. For the rest of the summer all I did was carry water, bucket by bucket to where the ground was too high for irrigation ditch water to flow.

"That farmer was so excited when the tassels turned to silk. He said the corn was almost ready. A couple of weeks later just before the harvest, that crazy coot sent me back. He told the miserable old couple that I 'didn't work out', and that I 'hadn't been any help to him at all, just a burden'. A blasted lie it was... yup an out-right blasted lie.

"Anyhow, early the next spring, or more exactly, late in winter around February when it was still bitter cold, an Old Basque Sheepherder named Fernando won the bid for my services. I spent the next month babysitting ewes 24-hours a day and alerting the Old Man when one of them went into labor.

"At that point he would spring into action to assure that each and every lamb was born alive and healthy. I'll be damned if them ewes didn't squirt out twins or triplets most all the time. I never knew such a thing. For 3 to 5 days we would have to keep check on all the little families of sheep to make sure that none of the lambs got abandoned from their mothers.

" 'Every lamb counts.' Fernando would say in his broken English, 'Every little one.' he would always repeat.

"We spent the spring and summer tending sheep. I learned how to dock a lamb, chase off predators, mark a bad ewe to be culled from the flock and how to move the sheep from meadow to meadow.

"Fernando said I was almost as good a hand as his 'Ole dog Shep' but I ate too much and moved too slow.

"Once in a while, a lamb might break a leg or otherwise be in peril. With solemnness and thanks to God, Fernando would sacrifice the fluffy little body and prepare a dinner of lamb for us.

"I was a bit hesitant to try it, but it only took one bite to convince me that maybe these Basque Sheepherder Folks had something going on there.

"One day an old ewe was molested by a wolf. She was a big ole gal and broke loose but started to run and ran herself right off a cliff. Being one to never waste a thing, Fernando scaled down the mountainside to her. He found her with 2 broken legs and had to put her out of her misery.

"I thought that was the end of that, but that crazy old man insisted I ascend down the cliff and help him drag her up, where he proceeded to dress her out and carve out a leg roast to bake in his dutch oven.

Old Joe

"Let me tell you friends, 'fried lamb' and an 'old ewe roast' are two totally different things. I could hardly gag her down. Seeing the uncertainness in my consumption of the ewe, Fernando directed me to 'chow it down as is, put some more garlic on it, or go without.' I went without. Shep was well fed that night.

"Come fall we moved the herd down the mountain to a makeshift corral, shipped the lambs off to market by railway and Fernando sent me packing back to the orphanage.

"I had grown to love and respect this man, but I knew I had no choice but to return.

"The old dastardly duo did not welcome me back. I consoled myself by believing that Fernando would be back in February to get me again."

Joe paused, he was visibly upset, clearing his throat he continued on...

"Fernando never returned. I learned years later that he had been killed that very winter trying to protect the herd from a famished grizzly bear who didn't have enough sense to sleep out the winter.

"As luck would have it, those two geezers became more and more abusive to me. A day hardly went by that I didn't' feel the swat of a broom, buggy whip or the slap of a hand.

"Wouldn't wish that kinda' life on my worst enemy."

After another hesitant silence, Joe returned to his narration.

"When the next potential savior arrived at the orphanage door, one of the other boys who had succumbed to the old man's whip more times than he could count, locked me in the outhouse in a desperate attempt to move himself to the top of the availability list.

"After menial effort to find me for presentation to the potential employee, the other boy was given the opportunity.

"I never did hold a grudge against him though. I might have done the same thing if I thought it would have gotten me out of that horrible situation one day sooner.

"I heard he ended up on a farm and eventually had a little place of his own with a wife and nine kids. Must have married him one of those Mormon gals I guess, funny how things work out."

JoAnn Nyman

A KIND HOME

Joe shot Josie half a smile and a snicker, then shaking his head he moved on with his story.

"After that incident, I spent more than a year with that miserable pair before an Irishman named MacKerry showed up looking for a possible blacksmith apprentice.

"I remember I couldn't pack my extra shirt and my little cedar box of personal trinkets fast enough to get out of that place.

"As I was leaving and had just passed through the gate out of that Hellhole, the old man stormed out of the house.

"He snatched my shirt and box away from me and bellowed, 'What do you think you are doing there you little thief? You don't own that stuff. Get out of here you ingrate.'

"MacKerry, saint as he was, stepped in between us. He doubled up his left hand into a solid fist and decked the old man. Hit him right on the chin he did, knocked him stone cold scattering my box and its contents across the yard.

"I grabbed my box and what items I could find on the ground and we took off like a Black Bat outa' Hell."

Remembering the event, Joe grinned with delight before he moved on with his tale.

"MacKerry and his wife Maureen worked me from sun-up to sun-down six days a week. The sabbath was reserved for rest, church services and praise for the Lord. They were good hard-working Christians and I felt like family.

"Maureen taught me how to read and write and MacKerry educated me in all aspects of horses.

"He showed me how to train a horse to drive, break a horse to ride, pack a pannier, diagnose a lame horse, wrap a shin splint, cushion a bruised frog, mend a cracked hoof and shoe anything with hooves.

"It was a good time in my life. Learned a lot. First time I ever felt like I belonged or like anybody cared.

Joe paused momentarily then added, "First time I ever witnessed true love."

His words floated off into the distance. After a bit of uneasy silence, Joe started up again with his story, "By and by, in life, things happen..."

MOVING ON

"When Joshua, who was MacKerry's teenage nephew arrived from the old country I realized it was time to relocate. MacKerry had another mouth to feed now and a new apprentice to train.

"Before they got around to asking me to move on, I announced to them that I thought I needed to explore other options in my life. I didn't know where I was going but I did know I wasn't going back to that damn Orphanage.

"Maureen cried, I guess she had grown a bit of affection for this ugly mug of mine. MacKerry solemnly nodded in agreement and finally requested that I stay on for another month or so.

"He wanted to get his nephew up to speed and asked if I could finish putting a hand on a 3-year-old grey well-bred mare he had purchased from an Englishman.

"It was a hard month. Every day I realized I was one day closer to being on my own. I was apprehensive to say the least. About a week before I was to leave, MacKerry took an unaccustomed and unexpected trip to a neighboring town. He was gone all day and into the night.

"When I asked Maureen where he was and what business he might have there, she just brushed me off and began spouting off a list of chores for me to do yet that day.

"She had never been abrupt with me before, and in my surprised state, I just walked out and spent some time brushing that grey mare."

Joe stopped his story and motioned for Josie to get him a cup of coffee. Katie was up and halfway to the pot before Josie gathered her feet up underneath herself. Some of the audience shuffled a bit and repositioned their seats, but nobody left the campfire.

J.J. reached around behind the stump he was sitting on and grabbing three medium sized logs, he strategically placed them on the fire. After topping off Joe's cup, Katie returned the pot to its warming rock, and sat down cross-legged in front of Matt.

Katie and Josie gazed at Joe. The boys and elder men looked at the fire.

Joe cautiously took a sip of the hot brew, cupped his hands around the cup and resumed talking, directing his words to the fire, not making eye contact with anybody in particular.

"It wasn't long before my 30-days was up. I announced at dinner one Friday night that I'd be heading out Monday at daybreak. Saturday was the longest day of my life.

"Under pretense of putting the final touch on that mare I saddled her up for one last ride and made an exceptionally long trip around the foothills, all the way to town and back. I tried to concentrate on the job at hand.

"Back at the cabin, MacKerry and Maureen avoided me and kept busy with menial chores.

"We all spent Sunday together, going to church and having a fried chicken picnic near the creek. We laughed and joked and pretended that nothing was wrong.

"When evening came, some neighbors, I forget their names now, came by and brought some whiskey. It was the only time I ever saw MacKerry take a drink. Needless to say, drink he did, and when the neighbor brought out his fiddle and rosined up his bow Joshua danced us an Irish Jig.

"We continued to be delighted when MacKerry and Maureen danced an Irish Waltz for us. Before long, we were all dancing and singing."

Shaking his head and laughing to himself Joe added, "Whiskey will do that to a man you know."

The crowd laugh and nodded in agreement. Joe took a couple of sips of his coffee, set the cup aside, took in a big breath of air and went along with his story.

"Anyway, Monday morning rolled around, and I gathered my little box. I sat on the edge of my cot and wondered when and where I might actually have a place to call home again.

"Out in the kitchen I could hear Maureen humming an Irish Waltz as she prepared breakfast. I'd have to admit I was slightly offended at her joyfulness, and quite frankly, a bit put-off.

"I had hoped to be able to just pass through the kitchen with a quick nod and goodbye, but that was not to be. MacKerry and Maureen were up and waiting for me. When I sat down for my last meal I was filled with sadness. The sparkle in the eyes of the Irish couple astonished and confused me.

"Tentatively sitting in my customary spot, I finally blurted out, 'What is wrong with you two?'

"Maureen couldn't control herself any longer. 'Tell him, husband, tell him right now before I burst!'

"MacKerry laughed a big boisterous laugh. 'Hold yur horses laddie, we've got a couple surprises for you.'

"Maureen reached under the edge of the red checkered tablecloth onto the seat of a chair hidden from view and pulled out a bundle.

"She excitedly handed it to me, and I swiftly opened the brown package. It contained a full set of new clothes, head to toe, two pair of socks, and a coat. I felt like a king and never imagined such a treasure.

"Before I had a chance to get over the shock of new clothes, MacKerry produced a new pair of store-bought boots and a genuine Stetson cowboy hat. I had never had anything so beautiful. I had never even had anything that wasn't handed down from someone.

"I remember jumping up and hugging MacKerry in tears.

" 'Get a hold boy.' He said to me. 'Blubber your tears on me wife, they is all from her, 'twas the missus idea don't ye know?'

"I turned my attention to Maureen and wrapped my arms around her and sobbed. When I had composed myself, we ate a hardy breakfast of sausage and fried potatoes.

"Maureen gathered up some jerky, a couple of day-old biscuits. some potatoes, a small sack of coffee and a pint of dried beans for my journey.

"Soon it was time to be on my way. As I was trying to wrap up my belongings into a nap sack. Joshua came in with a leather saddlebag. 'It ain't new,' he stuttered, 'but don't 'spect I'll have need of this any time in the near future. Might come in handy for ye.'

"I began to decline his offer but realized it sure would be easier to travel with some sort of tote over my shoulder. So, after a short moment of hesitation, I thanked him and packed up my new clothes and what few possessions I had gathered in my life.

"Heading for the door, I felt like a criminal headed for the gallows. I didn't even know which way I was 'gonna turn when I got to the garden gate.

"I hadn't noticed that MacKerry had headed outside while I was packing until I reached the door. I figured he was out to the barn doing chores. I was right.

"When we stepped into the morning sun, I could hear the old Irishman calling my name. I thought he must want a private goodbye without Maureen around to leak tears all over us. I set down my bags and stepped into the barn.

"MacKerry was standing there softly brushing the mane of the grey mare. She was saddled and bridled. He reached up, tucked her forelock behind the browband and gave her a pat.

"Turning his face away from me, he reached behind his back with the reins in his hand. Handing them to me he said, 'You might just as well take her with ye too Lad. She's just taking up room 'n the barn and she eats like a bloomin' pig she does.'

"She's a good little lassie and she'll do right by ya if you treat her like a lady. I can't afford her. Maureen 'as tucked a bill of sale into the pocket of y'ur new shirt, so there won't be no questions about a scrawny young'un like yourself sportin' a fancy well bread pony as she is.'

Joe interrupted his own story with a chuckle, "That's how Little Lassie got her name, good 'ol Little Lassie." Pausing momentarily, he nodded to himself as he stared into the fire. After a moment of silence, Joe continued.

"MacKerry told me, 'Y'ur a good boy Lad, and I wish ye the best all life has to offer ye. Maybe someday ye be as blessed as I 'ave been to 'ave your own Maureen, and a few little brats o' yur own to raise. Don't back talk me now Lad. You ain't never yet and this ain't the time to start. Grab them saddle bags and be off with ye.'

Joe's voice quivered, "I don't recall what happened after that, next thing I remember was riding that mare out the gate. Maureen called out to me some Irish blessing ditty about the road, the wind, the sunshine and the rain.

"I was 100-yards down the road when MacKerry ran up behind me. "Joe, we love ye Lad, make us proud. If ye 'appen ta find yurself 2 days ride due east of here, at the JR Bar ranch looking for a job, ye tell the man in charge I sent ye, he'd be watchin' fur ye, 'tis all set up ye know, 'is name be Wilf, if ye be a mind that 'tis. God speed Lad!"

Joe looked up to the sky, searching for the next words.

JoAnn Nyman

LIFE AT THE JR BAR

"That's how I ended up here. Didn't know straight up about a cow. But I learned. No story there, I'm just like everyone of you, I learned.

"I had that mare for 16 years, now I'm ridin' her daughter, but that ain't no story either, it just is."

Joe dropped his eyes down to the fire. J.J. reached for a log and passed it to Billy who placed it and a couple more onto the glowing coals.

After a long silence, Josie cleared her throat. Before she could say anything, Joe waved her away with a flick of his wrist.

"I guess none of all that malarkey makes any explanation as to the question you asked me last night does it?"

Answering his own question, he followed up, "I'm getting to it… ya, I'm getting to it. You got to understand the background before you can appreciate the situation."

Joe's spectators young and old looked at each other. They had become so enthralled in his story, that they had completely forgotten what Josie's inquiry initially was.

MARY KATE'S ARRIVAL

"Any ways…" Joe resumed, "I'd been here at the JR Bar for three or four years, I forget which, when Mary Kate rode in. Strange for a gal all alone to be traveling like that. She was on a rangy worn out sorrel gelding. He looked like he might have been an okay mount in his day but had obviously seen better days.

"Mary Kate's hair was all tied and tucked up under her hat. We all thought her to be an undernourished boy at first. She was wearing several layers of clothing to conceal her womanly traits.

"When she neared camp, 'n called out, 'Hello to camp!' and asked if she could share our fire; every hand stood to welcome that beautiful voice with the Irish accent. Most of the men had never heard such a tranquil sound. To me it was the sound of an Angel.

"Mary Kate had been traveling for a few days and welcomed the chance to have some company, just possibly a decent meal and with luck, a job opportunity.

"Our camp cook at that time was an older roundish Spanish Senora by the name of Juanita, she wasn't much of a cook, but she kept tabs on the boys, and none of us starved to death or got sick too often.

"I suspect Wilf kept Juanita around for her other skills and duties," Joe looked at Wilf and added. "No offence Boss."

Wilf, smiling as he pictured Juanita in his mind, nodded in agreement, "None taken Joe. You may just be telling the truth there."

The seasoned hands laughed out loud. The novice crew blushed and tried to hide their snickers.

Joe continued, "Juanita was up in an instant from where she crouched washing dishes and welcoming Mary Kate. Without asking, Juanita scooped up a big bowl of leftover stew. Mary Kate ate like she had been without substanance for some time.

"There was an immediate connection between those two. Next thing we knew, Mary Kate had joined the camp.

"Juanita was glad to have the female company. I imagine Juanita was instrumental in making that happen. Wilf always did let that woman talk him into things."

"Wilf butted in, "Well she was a lot easier to get along with when she was happy, and besides she liked to show her appreciation in real nice ways."

Virgil spoke up, "Maybe we could hear some of your stories about Juanita Boss?"

Wilf shook his head, "Not tonight boys. Besides Joe's relationship with Mary Kate is a lot more interesting... well maybe not as exciting or entertaining; but definitely more special. You go on Joe."

Joe began again, "Well Mary Kate and I became best friends and our friendship turned into more than that.

"I remember that first kiss we had, sitting on a log near a lake under a blanket of a million stars on a hot late summer's night. I was madly in love with her and she with me I suppose.

"It was there, that day, that I felt as though all was right in the world. I remembered the words MacKerry had spoken to me, and I realized that I was as blessed as a man could be.

"It wasn't long before the previous dreams we individually had, became aspirations united for a shared life.

"I figured it was time to hang up my identity as a solo rider and get hitched as a team. Ya know there is nothing quite like watching a pair of well broke horses workin' together, and with the good Lord as our double tree, I reckoned that we'd be just about able to pull any load this world had to dump on us.

"Together we devised a plan. You know… a spread of our own, a little cabin, a milk cow for cream, chickens for fresh eggs, a little garden full of potatoes and of course some kids. I wanted two kids, Mary Kate wanted twelve."

Joe laughed out loud, "We settled on five. A full house that would be… yup a full house.

"Anyway, we decided that after the fall round up, Mary Kate would take all of our summer wages and set off to find us a place where we could homestead and hopefully, she would have enough cash to put a down payment on a piece of property.

"The bonus I'd get from Boss for sticking out the winter would get us the provisions we would need to set up our own home come spring.

"She planned on spending the winter months in town, with any luck she could find some employment and a small inexpensive room to rent for the time being, which would leave any wages available to cash away for our future.

"My heart ached the day she left. Throughout the winter my anticipation of her return and our future together grew by the day."

Joe suddenly stopped talking and fixed his eyes on the dwindling fire.

JoAnn Nyman

MARY KATE

After a moment of silence, Josie hesitantly asked, "What was she like Joe?"

Joe looked up towards the night sky. The half-moon over head was shining down upon the assembled troop. Stars filled the heavens.

The logs on the fire cracked and spit, oozing pine gum down their sides that quickly sizzled away.

Joe was slow to speak what was so very deeply etched into his heart and mind.

"Awe..." he crooned, "She was a beauty. Her smile could warm the heart of the devil. Her long and wavy hair hung clear to her waist and was the most beautiful auburn color imaginable, like a beeswax-shined chestnut.

"Her eyes were green and sparkled although they could pierce clean thru you if she even suspected a bit of sarcasm or a possible fib. There was a rainbow of freckles across her little nose that spilt over onto her cheeks just above two perfectly centered dimples.

"Her hands were remarkable, she could cook anything, taught Juanita a thing or two. Had a talent to be able to turn the most meager fixin's into a feast for a king. She could sew fine fancies as good as any woman, mend britches, canvas, tents, harnesses and tack, complete with fancy tooling and fine stitchin'.

"Mary Kate believed it was easier to keep things in good repair than to fix things up after a bad wreck.

"She was courageous and daring but never reckless. She spoke her mind, and sometimes was a little too outspoken. Mary Kate never intentionally hurt anyone or anything, but her impulsiveness caused her to be quite proficient in delivering apologies.

"She could paint a sunset or draw a scene like that Charlie Russel feller. Her penmanship rivaled that of any school marm and she could work numbers as well as any bookkeeper dreamed of doing. She prized wild raspberries, choke cherry jelly and biscuits.

"Don't anybody here dare think them hands weren't hard workers. Mary Kate was as good a hand as any man on this spread. Not as strong of course, but she worked smart. Those hands were more than gifted when working with livestock and could calm a balky colt, identify a hot spot on a lame horse, or help a young heifer deliver her 1st calf with ease.

"She was damn determined, and she never quit a job until it was complete. Patient and caring with all animals, she never did "break" a horse, but rather, she coaxed and trained it into submission. Horses wanted to work for her.

"To Mary Kate, everything in life was a grand adventure. She had a great sense of humor and enjoyed setting up harmless tricks to pull on others. She saw the good in everybody and was always helping others.

"She was generally patient, but once the patience wore thin, you better watch out, that fiery red-headed gal could become right uppity.

"Mary Kate could sing a hymn that would make songbirds stop and take notice. She appreciated all of God's beauty around us. She loved wildflowers and knew their names. Lavender and purple columbine were her favorite. Green was her favorite color."

Joe snickered to himself remembering. "She always said, 'Green goes with everything, ever see a wildflower that didn't look respectable with green leaves?' Then she would laugh uncontrollably at herself."

Joe smiled at recollecting her silliness, shook his head and moved on.

JoAnn Nyman

"Mary Kate collected things from nature, a strand of mane from a favorite horse, dried leaves, pretty rocks and shards of wood with fascinating patterns or colors of woodgrain.

"She believed in and collected an odd array of good luck charms but mostly, she was a God-fearing woman, and faith in the Lord that things would always work out.

"She knew and understood the words of the Lord. She spoke of the atoning sacrifice of Jesus for each of us. She treasured the poetry of the Psalms and had many of them memorized.

"Mary Kate believed in fate and that things always happened for a reason. She believed in angels and in the strength and power of love.

"She was the love of my life she was.

"Nevertheless, come springtime she never returned. No word. Nothing." Joe spoke quietly with unmistakable sadness in his voice, "For two years I watched and waited. For two years I wanted to go after her. For two years I wallowed in self-pity.

"I was afraid to find out the truth. I figured Mary Kate had changed her mind. Or maybe a terrible accident had come upon her. Maybe she found somebody who could give her more than I had to offer.

"Some of the boys suggested that maybe our relationship was all a ploy and she had played me for a fool. I knew in my heart that scenario was not the case. In my little box, with my keepsakes, I had a few items she left with me for safe keeping. Nobody who was trying to pull the wool over somebody's eyes would have done that. And besides I felt that I knew her heart, and she just wasn't like that."

JOE'S STORY CONTINUES AS WILF MAKES A DECLARATION

"After two years of brooding like an old red hen, Boss came to me."

Looking at Wilf, Joe asked, "Remember what you said to me that day?"

Wilf shrugged his shoulders, "Not exactly, but I sure recall the jest of the conversation."

The cow hands sniggered.

Joe went ahead with his story, "Well Boss, you told me; 'Joe you're no good to me in this awful state. You got your head way up your… well, up in the clouds my boy, and it's time you quit pining over that little red-headed Irish gal. You better take a month off, go find that green-eyed lassie and get things settled.' Then ya told me,

" 'Here's your pay to date and a month in advance. If I don't see ya in 30 days, I'll know ya aint coming back and you don't owe me a thing. Call it a wedding gift or a dowry to start a new life in a new place, whatever the case may be.' "

Wilf nodded in agreement, "Yup, sounds like something I'd say."

Joe looked at his pocket watch and was about to offer an excuse for not continuing on when Wilf spoke up again, "Boys, I've made a decision, Indian summer is dragging on with mild weather, there's plenty of feed here in this little valley I think we'll not move camp for a day or two."

"Tomorrow is Sunday and you have all earned a day of rest. Maybe some of you could clean up a bit in the creek in the morning, check out your tack, give your mounts a good brush down and write your mom or sweethearts a letter."

Young and old started ribbing one another. It had been a long time since they had a day off. Most of them had no idea what day of the week it really was, but if Wilf said tomorrow was gonna be Sunday than tomorrow was gonna be Sunday.' Joe's defense for calling it a night had just sailed out the window.

Virg stood and approached the fire. With the corner of his apron in hand, he checked the coffee pot. After looking into the swirling sludge, he reconsidered pouring himself a cup and set the pot aside.

Old Joe

When the excitement of the ensuing holiday simmered down, the congregation around the campfire grew quiet once again. All eyes focused on Joe. He poked a stick at a stray log laying on the outskirts of the flames and rolled it into the center of the fire. After a few seconds of smoking and smoldering the bulky stump burst into a flame.

JoAnn Nyman

JOE'S SEARCH FOR MARY KATE

"Well," Joe said, clearing his throat, "go to town I did. I described Mary Kate as best I could to every soul I came across along the way. One woman in a mercantile thought she sounded familiar but the gal she remembered was obviously married.

"Another woman remembered a traveling gal with ginger hair but didn't think it could be Mary Kate 'cuz the gal she remembered was a bit on the 'chunky' side.

"The next town or two that I searched turned up no clues at all. A couple of days later in a little Podunk-hole of a place, the blacksmith remembered Mary Kate's horse.

"He said her sorrel gelding had a bad shoe he had reset for her and thought she had headed further west. So west I went, but I lost her trail. Just when I was about to give up, a barkeeper provided me with a bit of hope.

"He believed by my description, that Mary Kate sounded similar to a gal he'd talked to who had been looking for a doctor. I found out that there were no doctors within a hundred miles of that place, and I was at a dead-end again when a soiled dove from the local saloon suggested that I try asking a gal by the name of 'Sylvia Jane'.

"Sylvia Jane, I found out, was an old negro woman who lived in a sod-house in the side of a hill a little way from town. It didn't click right away in my mind that Sylvia Jane was a midwife and that's how come all the professional ladies knew her, and it didn't occur to me that Mary Kate had need of a midwife. Guess I'm just a bit dense in the head at times.

Old Joe

"When I finally tracked down Sylvia Jane and inquired about Mary Kate, I still couldn't believe that the woman Sylvia Jane was telling me about was my Mary Kate. It was only after she produced a tattered dusty letter that Mary Kate had written to me that I actually believed it was her."

Joe's words came slowly now, "Mary Kate had been with child… my child… I never knew…had no idea… never thought.

"In the letter, Mary Kate told me she had named our child after me and she prayed that the name would serve well and hopefully help us to be able to find each other someday.

"The note talked about our time together; said she loved me more everyday than the day before. Told me she would be watching over me and our child until we were reunited at Saint Peter's Gate.

"She said she'd be waiting; but not to be in a hurry because there were things I needed to do yet on earth before we could be in Eternity together."

No one spoke a sound, most looked away as if loss of eye contact would somehow give Joe space and reverence.

After a moment of silence Joe rubbed his nose as though a knat was pestering him, then he proceeded. "Sylvia Jane said Mary Kate was a trouper, did everything right but in the end, Sylvia Jane just couldn't save her. Nope she just couldn't save her." Joe's voice faded off into a whisper.

More silence followed. Josie was just about to ask about the baby when Joe cleared his throat. He murmured, "Sylvia Jane saved our baby's life but she didn't have the inclination nor the means to raise a child, especially a white baby."

Sniffing, and rubbing his nose, Joe pressed on, "Sylvia Jane passed off what she believed to be an orphan to a Christian family with seven or eight kids of their own.

"She didn't know what had happened to them folks but said she had heard they might'a moved on with a bunch of settlers looking for some promised land out west.

"Just as I thought my life had come to an end and I could take no more of Sylvia Jane's story, she said she had heard that them Christians took second thought and had left our baby in some orphanage somewhere.

"After what Hell my life had been being raised in an orphanage and all, I was devastated to think about my child... our child being raised in an institution like that."

Joe paused to compose himself. His audience waited in silence.

JoAnn Nyman

BACK AT MacKERRY'S

"I was feeling pretty low by then, so I made a side trip to see Maureen and MacKerry. When I crested the top of the hill so that I had a clear shot at their place I was dumbfounded. The spit and polished homestead I remembered was in a bad state of disarray. I went to investigate anyway.

"I found their Joshua doing the best he could to keep things together. But Maureen and MacKerry were gone. He said they went west to California when they heard about the gold rush.

"I couldn't believe they were chasing after gold. Joshua corrected me, by telling me that they were not chasing gold, they were shoeing horses for all those miners. Now that made more sense. Anyway, he hadn't heard from them for months.

"Before I had a chance to tell him about Mary Kate, he wanted to know if I received my gift. I didn't know what he was talking about, and he said, 'Well that's too bad, never mind, so what brings you to these parts anyway? You on a social call?'.

"I was so consumed about finding my and Mary Kate's baby that I never pushed him for more information about some (gift) as he called it.

"I began telling him all about Mary Kate and my search for her and now for our baby. Midpoint in my account, MacKerry's nephew got a green look about him. He put a hand up over his face. With his other hand he waved wildly at me to stop talking and slumped into a chair sitting there on the porch.

"When he finally composed himself, Joshua spoke in a whimper, 'So ye did get our gift. Mary Kate's me sister. We sent her alookin' for ye. MacKerry figured ye'd be at the JR bar'.

"I plopped down on the edge of the porch speechless. I had no idea. My only guess as to her reason for not revealing who she was, could be wanting our relationship to stand on its own merit, But I guess I'll never know…At least not in this life."

Joe's voice floated off into the air. Aware of the silence, he began again, "Anyway… I spent the night, and as Mary Kate's brother had no information to add to my knowledge, come morning I was back on the road.

"Little Lassie and I were not five minutes down the road when a down pour burst upon us. It drenched us continually for 3 days and nights. I've never been more physically and emotionally distraught than I was right then.

THE CONVENT

"My last hope was to track down that child. I spent the next two weeks traveling from town to town. When I finally came upon an old fort that had been turned into a makeshift convent.

"There must have been a hundred strays living in that place. In speaking with the nuns, I derived that most of the children living there were dropped off in the dead of night near the garden gate.

"People would just leave them there, ring the bell and disappear into the night. When the nuns would hear the bell, they knew the Lord had brought to them another charge.

"Sometimes the babies had a note pinned to their blanket with their given name, more often, the nuns would christen the children with a name, possibly from the Bible that they felt inspired to assign.

"Sometimes they would just start calling the child by some short nickname, let a foster family come up with a name or let the kids pick their own name when they left to be on their own.

"It wasn't such a good system, but God bless those nuns, they did the best they could do.

"It was a full-time job for all those saintly women just taking care of the physical needs of all those bereaves.

"Keeping records of when little ones arrived and whether or not they possessed a name upon arrival or were named afterwards were incomplete to say the least.

"There were five children there in what I guessed to be the correct age group, that I singled out that could have been Mary Kates and mine. Five kids with no surname. Five kids toddling around with no apparent mother or father.

Old Joe

"I had no way of knowing for sure if one of them was ours, and if so, which one that might be.

"I was partly relieved and extremely thankful that the nuns were nothing like the people I had been left with but saddened that any child had to grow up without a mother or a father."

JoAnn Nyman

A DECADE ROLLS ON

"I gave the nuns what money I had, and in an attempt to get on with this tale I'll condense the next 12 or so years.

"I kept on here at the JR Bar and squirreled away every dime I could.

"I didn't know anything else to do, and Wilf was more than lenient letting me have time off when he could.

"Two or three times a year I would visit that convent, donate as much of my wages as I could and spend a day or two helping out. There always seemed to be a roof to fix or some other chore I could assist with.

"Them visits were like a ray of sunshine mid a month-long downpour. My life for all them years revolved around planning one trip to the next.

"Every time I went, I got to know all the kids at the convent a little better, but I focused on five in particular. Many of the other kids came and went but not that handful of little ones I had my eye on.

"I knew it was only a matter of time before they would be sent out to fend for themselves as well. I knew that when that happened, I would never be able to keep track of them.

"Funny they never got 'dopted out...I guess Mary Kate was right about God working in mysterious ways and heavenly angels and all that.

"Every trip I took caused me to realize that I was rolling the dice and that one day my luck was bound to run out and one or more of them kids would be lost to me, maybe even all of 'em. That's when I decided something had to be done.

ROUNDING UP THE STRAYS

"It took a lot a courage for me to ask Boss if I could bring one back to the JR Bar to hire on as a new hand.

"That's right," Wilf interjected, "you should have seen him solicit the case for the need of a helper around here. I reckoned that if I didn't give in, I'd be out a good hand. I figured I had invested too many years just getting Joe to learn how to throw a rope to give up on him now.

"The older hands laughed out loud and slapped their knees. They all knew Joe was the best man on the ranch with a rope whether heading, healing, afoot or horseback."

"Before the laugher had a chance to wear itself out, Joe resumed, "With that being said, knowing Boss wasn't too keen on the idea, I headed out to the convent once more.

"I was sure that this trip would mark the definitive decision of my life. I had spent years trying to determine which, if any of that hand full of youngsters was, or could possibly be my flesh and blood.

"Every trip I had taken I came away with a different feeling. I saw things within each one that led me to believe that they were the one I was searching for.

"I was at the convent for 5 days when Sister Sarah came to me. With her sympathetic understanding voice, she asked, 'What is troubling you my son?'

"After I had sufficiently detailed my story and dilemma to her, Sister Sarah advised, 'Only the Lord can answer your questions... only the Lord. Ask in faith young man, and you shall receive and answer.'

"I retreated to the chapel and 'poured my heart out unto the Lord' as one might say. For hours I contemplated every aspect of my life's choices, the short time with Mary Kate, and the things I had witnessed among the five orphans before me. I pondered, and deliberated.

"If you're thinking you are about to hear a story about an angel or heavenly messenger come down from up above to give me guidance, you would be mostly wrong. Although what I experienced was heaven sent.

"It took a long time for this old thick head of mind to accept the premonitions that kept popping into my mind. My memories of Mary Kate kept circling back to that day and night we spent dawdling on the edge of a meadow alongside a clear cool creek.

"In my mind I repeated our conversation from that day over and over. All I could absolutely remember with perfect recollection was our discussion about kids. Me wanting two, and her hoping for a dozen. I could hear her voice over and over telling me. 'Okay Joe, we'll settle on five.' "

Joe stopped in mid-thought then he repeated gently, " 'Okay Joe, we'll settle on five.' Those were the words that kept repeating in my head over and over. Those were the words the angels were whispering to my mind and heart, over and over and over…

"That's when I knew what I had to do; never imagined for a minute that Boss would go along with my cockamamie idea, but I thought it couldn't hurt to ask.

"I spent every minute on that return trip preparing myself to have to say goodbye to the JR Bar. I was wishing Juanita was still around to help me out coercing Boss into giving me and my scroungy mob a chance."

Joe shook his head from side to side, "Boys you should have seen Wilf's face when I came into camp with that old supply wagon filled with five ratty lookin' scrawny kids. Three boys and two little girls to boot. I thought he was gonna pop a cork right then and there. Never heard a man go off about somebodies crazy, foolish, half-baked idea quite like Boss did that day. He finally just threw his good hat on the ground and stomped off.

"After an hour or so, I went looking for him. He was sitting on a log overlooking a big deep canyon kinda' talking to himself saying over and over, 'No, nope, not gonna happen, nope, no way'. When I figured it was safe to approach, I just sat down easily on the far end of the log. 'I know you said one Boss, it ain't that I can't count, it's just that I can't elect which one that it ought to be.'

"As if that was the end-all to the conversation, Boss said, 'I don't have funds to pay that many hired hands.' I told him, 'We just need a place to be, a roof overhead come winter and 2 good meals a day.'

"Wilf still wasn't on board, were ya boss?"

Wilf fervently shook his head no. "Not one bit, All I could see was troubles times five." He interjected still ardently shaking his head no as Joe continued, "Well, I finally got him to agree to a six-week trial period."

"Never for the life of me did I think you all would work out six days let alone six weeks." Wilf expressed.

"Ya know, come to think of it Boss, we never did have another discussion after that."

"Lord a mighty," Wilf said, "Anyway Joe, how come you never come to me after the six weeks so we could make a plan and a decision?"

Looking embarrassed and a bit sheepish, Joe replied, "Figured it was just best to keep them kids busy and on the straight and narrow and maybe you wouldn't notice they was still hanging around"

Virgil jumped in with his own opinion on that matter, "Well I damn sure noticed they were still here. Them five rascals eat more vittles than ten grown men, I can hardly keep enough biscuits, beans and bacon around here to keep 'em all quiet."

The men all laughed exuberantly. Katie and Josie tried to feign insult but began to giggle themselves. J.J. and Billy Joe ribbed each other and pointed their fingers at Matt whose height and weight showed that he wasn't afraid of Virg's seconds. Matt patted his tummy and shrugged.

Joe looked around at the jovial crowd. He was hoping that he could forgo the rest of his story.

Josie was not about to let that happen.

JOSIE'S QUERY REVISITED

Katie nudged Josie. "Joe…" softly said Josie, "We've been here at the JR Bar right near 2 years…"

Josie paused looking for the right words to ask Joe about his odd nightly behavior, but before she could compose a sentence Joe spoke up, "I guess that brings us up to your question then doesn't it? So, just what in the hell am I doing every night after supper?

"I'll tell you. What I do each night is for Mary Kate. I write her a letter, like the notes and letters she use to write to me

"At first, I use to just tell her how much I missed her and how much I loved her. But since all you strays have been here, I tell her about you. What you do and what you say. Just like I would do at the end of each day if she were back at home in that little cabin we talked about."

Joe fidgeted a bit; he was lost in thought and appeared unaware of the crowd listening to him. He spoke directly and intimately to Josie.

"I tell Mary Kate about Katie being a great help to Virg. Her painting, sewing, singing and her penmanship.

"I write to her about Matt's keeping things in good repair, his beautiful leatherwork and braiding, his tender hands, his tolerance, patience and sometimes his unruly impatience. And I always tell her about his latest Grand Adventure.

"I explain to Mary Kate how Billy Joe sees the good in everybody. I joke to her about how silly he looks when his too long, curly reddish-blond mane gets all wet. How his 'little-boy' looks, and freckles disguise the never-quit strength he displays. How his calm voice, composure and skill can turn a grave situation into a triumph. How he collects natures beautiful things, identifies wildflowers and how angels watch over him.

"I pen about J.J. and that damn good luck scarf, how he makes life fun and entertaining for all of us, how he always thinks of others and how he sneaks biscuits to enjoy mid-morning. Not to mention his habit of pulling tricks on unsuspecting victims.

"I describe the expertise I see in you Josie, when I watch you coerce a young horse into submission. The humility I see when I observe your prayer time. The passion I feel when I hear you recite your poetry. And the pride I have in you when your bravery causes you to stand up to Boss or me with a question.

"Mostly I tell her how proud I am of ALL of you, and how much I love her." Joe stopped and took a big deep breath.

"So…That's what I do each night. Nothing outstanding. Just write'n a few words about my day, my observations and my thoughts."

Joe took another big deep breath and let it out slowly. He coughed a bit and sniffed. Rubbing his nose, he looked around at the five young inquisitive faces.

Josie whispered, "You miss her don't you Joe?

"Hell yes I miss her! Damn right! But not like I did, not now… not now that I see her everywhere."

"You mean like a ghost or something?"

Joe snickered, "No, not like a ghost or spirit, but in a more tangible way than that."

"What do you mean?"

Joe's grin widened, "I see Mary Kate's smile every day on Katie's face. I see her green eyes each time I look at Matt. I see the sunlight dancing off her auburn hair when I look at you Josie, the sparkle of Mary Kates' mischievous eyes in J.J., and her freckles on Billy's dirty face.

"I hear Mary Kate when Katie sings, when Billy calms a frightened calf with his voice, when J.J. sets someone up for a joke, when Matt recites a grand adventure he has had and when you pray Josie.

"I remember Mary Kate when I watch the patience and gentle way Matt cares for animals and others.

"When I watch Katie, I recall how she saw the goodness in people and loved to do things for others and make the world around her beautiful and precise.

"I am reminded that Mary Kate loved good luck charms, anything green, and having fun, when I come across J.J. during my day.

"I think of her pluck, determination and thankfulness when I witness Billy Joe taking care of business."

"And you Josie, when I am near you, I feel her spirituality, faith, and love of God.

"That's what I write about and I send my words to Mary Kate thru the swirls and whirls of the campfires smoke.

"And that's my story. That's why I do what I do."

THE CEDAR BOX

"What about the box Joe? Was that the one you had in the orphanage?"

Sitting behind him throughout the evening's presentation was Joe's box. Joe leaned over and picked it up. He had nearly forgot that he had fetched it over to the campfire.

"Yes," he said, "Yes, it's the only thing I have from my childhood. Not sure where it came from. I guess it's all I've ever truly owned that wasn't a necessity. I had it to put special things in. It was pretty empty 'til Mary Kate came along."

Joe carefully folded open the lid to the cedar box and reached inside. He pulled out a scrap of blue flannel cloth. "That's all I got left of the blanket I was wrapped in when I arrived at the orphanage."

Replacing the cloth, Joe drew out another item. A dried-up crusty piece of leather. He dawned a disgusted look as he held it up to the mass. "This use to be a pig's ear." he said with a strange grimace on his face. Don't know why I ever kept it. I guess to remind myself how miserable pig farmers have it."

He dropped the ear and fished for another article. Holding up for all to view, Joe displayed a matted ball of wool. "This was fluffy and pure white at one time." he remarked. "It came off an old ewe that tried to kill me one night. I suppose she didn't realize that I was trying to help her."

Joe plopped the dirty wool back into the box.

The next thing Joe displayed was a small swatch of linen wrapped around a handful of seeds tied in a bundle with a piece of brown twine. "Wonder if this old corn seed would ever grow us an ear to eat?" he questioned.

Joe casually tossed the bundle into the container, stirring around in the box for a minute moving some yet unseen treasures out of the way.

He exclaimed, "Here it is!" as he triumphantly withdrew a horseshoe nail. "MacKerry told me to always keep one handy, never know when you might need it. Funny I've needed it plenty 'a times, but it was always back at camp or at the ranch when I needed it elsewhere."

"Suppose it didn't do me any good there." Joe said as he replaced the nail into the box and stared down into its darkness. His happy demeanor quickly transformed into soberness.

He picked up a handful of loose papers and a few tied together. "These here are a couple letters from Maureen and the bill of sale for that old grey mare I used to have. This little stack tied with red ribbon are poems, notes and letters from Mary Kate."

Joe slipped one page out from the others. It was folded neatly and precisely; first in half, then into thirds. "This is the note the nuns gave to me from Mary..." Joe paused, cleared his throat, "...my...Mary Kate."

With great reverence, Joe opened the note. The silence was deafening. For a moment it looked as though Joe was going to read the note out loud to his listeners, but it was not to be as he looked at it, then folded it up and replaced it under the ribbon on top of the little stack.

Still looking into the container, Joe spoke up, "Billy Joe, I think Mary Kate would want you to have this." He withdrew a small slice of an old cedar post. There within the intricate patterns of the grain appeared a miraculous wonder.

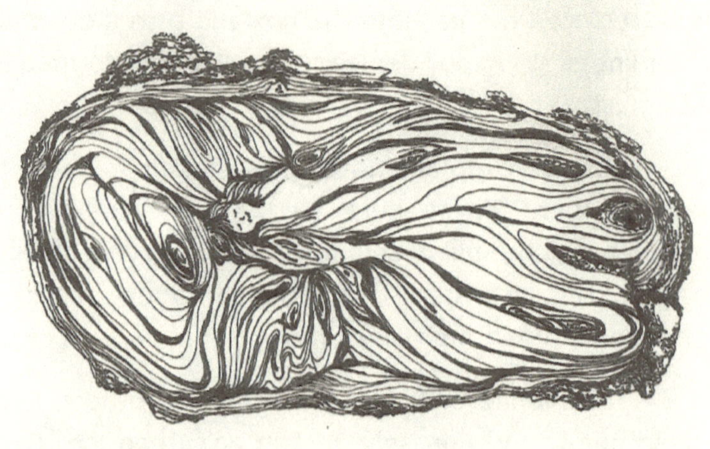

Joe held it towards the light of the fire. "Look here Billy, can you see the Angel in flight?"

Billy Joe stood and moved next to Joe. He took the tiny piece of timber and studied the design. After a moment his eyes began to water. He rubbed them and surveyed the slab again. Delight filled his face as he nodded in agreement. He drew the artifact to his chest, retreated to his seat and mumbled a tearful, "Thank you."

Joe gazed into the box. He looked at the faces around the fire anxiously awaiting his every word and action. "Katie," he said, "I'm sure you are meant to have this."

Katie approached Joe hesitantly as he handed her a glass inkwell and a fancy lettering pen. "You'll know what to do with this." he said.

Katie held the writing set as if it were a fragile robin's egg. "Oh my!" she exclaimed still in shock at seeing the lovely gift. "Thank you. Thank you, I do know what to do with it."

Katie returned to her place around the fire.

J.J. moved nervously in his seat then decided the fire needed another log or two. He raised up conspicuously, grabbed a handful of pine logs and placed them ceremoniously on the fire.

Joe shook his head; he wasn't the only one who could see through J.J.'s pretenses.

"Get over here." Joe directed, "Not that you need anything else for luck since you sport that obnoxiously big neckerchief day after day. Nonetheless I'm sure if Mary Kate were here, she would assign this to you."

Joe offered J.J. a seemingly empty trivial-looking leather coin purse. J.J. took it and with a puzzled look on his face, inspecting his prize he turned the wallet over and over.

"Look inside boy." Joe encouraged.

J.J. folded the little flap back and squeezing the sides of the flat container open, he peered inside. With a shake and a tap onto the palm of his hand a thin silver coin appeared. J.J. turned the coin over to reveal a four-leaf clover embossed upon the coin.

J.J.'s face lit up like the fourth of July. Every one of his freckles was stretched wide from the grin spread across his face. J.J. held the coin out for Billy Joe to see then securely placed it back into its holder and sat back down.

Everyone's attention was now focused back on Joe. Into the box again went his hand and he drew out a small booklet.

"Josie, this best be your bequest." Joe stated, with a matter of fact tone of voice, as though it could be of use to none of the others.

Josie took the booklet with both hands as if it were a delicate flower. She turned it over to reveal the wording on the front cover.

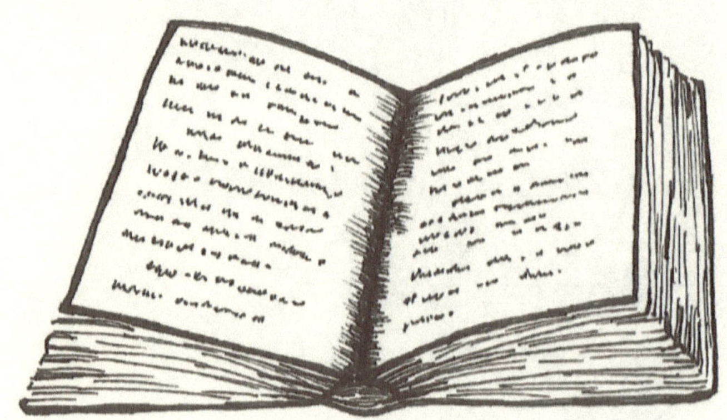

"The Psalms of David"

Overtaken with emotion, Josie clutched the book to her breast and nodding in agreement. Re-seated herself with tears streaming down her face.

Joe reached into the box one last time. "Matt," he jested, "I don't know what you would ever do with such a thing, but the only thing from Mary Kate that I have left in here for you is this..."

Joe passed to Matt a folded-up white cotton handkerchief. Matt spread it out across his lap, and unfurling it exposed a delicate cameo necklace. The background was a subtle shade of green, decorated with the image of a lovely young woman, her hair coiled high upon her head and ringlets gently cascading around her face.

Matt picked it up and inspected the broach more intently.

"Maybe someday you'll have a special someone in your life that you might want to present that to."

Matt smiled to himself, "Ya, maybe I will." he said, "Thank you. It's beautiful."

JoAnn Nyman

YEARS GO BY

Matt and Katie married and had a little spread not too much different than the one Joe and Mary Kate dreamed of complete with a garden of vegetables and flowers. They kept busy raising a few head of cattle, and for additional income, Matt hired out to do leather work and tack repairs.

Katie's artistry with pen and paint decorated their home from top to bottom, and she pocketed quite a bid of change selling her images at the local mercantile. They raised two green eyed children named Joseph and Mary Kate.

Josie stayed with the JR Bar, supervised the breeding and training of horses and ran the books for Wilf until he passed on. She married a traveling preacher who showed up to the JR bar every few weeks. He would spend some time with Josie, then he would be off. It was an odd arrangement, but Josie just couldn't leave the ranch and Joe.

Somewhere along the way, Josie and her preacher husband had a couple little girls and a little boy. All three of them donned Josie's auburn locks.

Billy Joe married Ellen Rose, a granddaughter of Wilf who bore 7 children for him in 12 years. That little herd of kids kept them both busy from sun-up to sundown.

Come springtime each year, Billy would do double duty overseeing the cow/calf operation on the JR Bar as well as general foreman over the entire ranch.

Billy had worked hard to earn his way to the top and the responsibility was given to him on merit, not due to his fortunate marriage.

Some of the cowboys pestered him about marrying Ellen Rose to gain the upper hand, but it was all in jest, as Billy was well admired and respected by every member of the ranch crew, young and old alike.

By the time he had reached 30, Billy's freckles ultimately tanned themselves out, but the apple never does fall too far from the tree, and despite Ellen's porcelain complexion, every one of Billy's seven kids displayed his trademark speckles across their noses and a hint of auburn in their hair.

J.J. took up cooking for the JR Bar and took over after Virgil had passed away in his sleep on a cold winters' night. Rumor has it that Virg was 92 years old and had cooked for at least 10 various outfits for over 70 years. He was sorely missed.

J.J. never did marry, although he always seemed to be courting two or more gals at a time. He said life was a lot more fun with women chasing you than he imagined settling down might be.

J.J. always had a good reason to go to town for supplies and seemed to make the trip a lot more often than Virgil ever did, and not nearly in as quick a time.

He could never get away from those dimples and bragged that those dimples, together with his red mustache, drove the ladies wild. J.J. never seemed to age, and most of his suitors were significantly younger than him although they had no idea of that fact. He continued to be the life of the party and to collect things from nature.

Mary Kate's brother, **Joshua** and Joe became quite close. He developed a rather well-known reputation for being the best blacksmith around.

Four or more times a year Joshua would arrive at the ranch with his wagon load of farrier supplies and reset shoes for all the cowboys for a fair price. The cowboys welcomed his expertise as they all knew the old adage, "No hoof, no horse."

Joe welcomed his visits and kept in contact with Maureen and MacKerry through the U.S. Post and Joshua.

And Joe... as this story is about; what happened to Joe?

Well, Joe, a humble, hardworking man of integrity and high character, lived his life on the JR Bar, content to be just a cowboy. A common man, mostly average in height and weight. A blue-eyed man with sandy blond hair that had turned rather greyish in his ageing years.

THE END

When Josie showed up at the little cabin of Matt and Katie mid-summer, they knew something was wrong. She was riding Tiny Lass, Little Lassie's newest granddaughter, an additional indication that something was not right. It would be a cold day in Hell before anyone at the ranch would even consider riding any of the offspring of Joe's mare.

Josie fell to the ground in her haste to dismount a horse that was still sliding to a stop. Matt was there in an instant with Katie by his side lifting Josie to her feet. Josie was nearly inconsolable, she clung onto Matt and Katie. Through tears and sobs she poured out her story.

"There had been an accident, a dreadful accident and in the end...

...in the end... Joe was gone.

That's all there was to it... He was gone."

Katie fell to her knees and the burden was now on Matt's shoulders to console both of the women. Not an easy task when your own heart is breaking...

Back at the ranch J.J. and Billy Joe were tending to the necessary arrangements and excavating a hole six feet deep into the ground.

Fittingly, it was on the edge of the meadow near the creek where Joe and Mary Kate had spent the day leisurely together, consummating their love for one another, so very many years ago.

It was here, basking in each other's affection, where Joe had unwillingly agreed to raise five children with Mary Kate, the love of his life.

Ellen Rose jogged her team down the dusty road to town in the supply wagon. Tears streamed down her cheeks.

Empty now, the wagon bed would soon contain a pine box and be headed back to the ranch to gather with the others. Ellen hoped she would be able to run down Joshua and Josie's husband and bring them back with her as well, as they would both be needed for support at this trying time.

THE FAREWELL

On the third day, at sunrise, the congregation met under the watchful eyes of five mature limber pines huddled together.

A stand of smaller golden aspens flanked either side of the cluster of pines. The morning breeze, working its way down the canyon, sang a mournful refrain softly. The heart-shaped buttery leaves of the aspens tinkled in the breath of the wind.

Wilf and Virg were the last to arrive driving the supply wagon. The draft team walked sluggishly and deliberate. The freshly oiled harnesses glistened in the sun.

Josie walked slowly behind the wagon leading Tiny Lass. The breeze gently tossed around the silver mane of the riderless mount. Usually high-headed and chomping at the bit, the young mare followed along, head hung down. She seemed to understand the solemnness of the occasion.

When the wagon finally came to a halt, Josie secured Tiny Lass to the back panel, gave her a pat on the neck and kissed her muzzle gently.

Wilf and Virg sat stoically for a time before unloading themselves and escorting Josie to the side of her husband.

The attendees gathered around the open grave. A simple pine box with an elaborate inset made of cedar indicating a family tree with five main branches and multiple smaller limbs, covered the top half of the lid.

Matt and Katie stood arm in arm with Little Joseph and Mary Kate clinging to their sides.

Billy Joe and Ellen Rose were standing to their right. Five older children crowded together beside them.

Old Joe

Billy stared at the casket as he patted the back of a toddler in his arms hoping to coax him off to sleep. Ellen swaddled a baby to her breast, looking back and forth from her kids to her husband and back to the baby once again.

J.J. was positioned to the left of Matt and Katie. The characteristic twinkle in his eyes was overshadowed by red and puffy bags. His dimples were in company of a rogue tear drop slowly rolling over his cheeks.

Three beautiful younger women stood behind J.J. with their outstretched hands resting upon his arm and shoulders.

Josie and her husband were positioned directly across from the others. The Preacher stood with Bible in one hand and his other arm around Josie's shoulder. Three children clung onto her skirt. Josie trembled.

Joshua, twenty-seven assorted ranch hands, and a dozen towns folk huddled around the perimeter of the gravesite.

Matt, Katie, Billy Joe, J.J. and Josie looked about to each other each giving the others a discreet nod of acknowledgement in agreement.

Josie nudged her partner to begin.

The Preacher cleared his throat three times to gain everyone's attention. Then he began, "With the exception of one late summers night, around a campfire long ago, Joe was a man of few words. That's the way he was. He thought that a man's actions were a better indication of a man's beliefs and convictions than idle talk.

"All of us here today know that fact for sure if we knew him at all. With that in mind, I'll not detract from the way I believe Joe would want these services to be.

"Joe wouldn't like me, nor anybody else rambling on and on. Joe would say, 'Just say what's what and move on".

"So I will... Joe was fair and honest. His story telling was mostly truthful and any exaggerations were just for entertainment purposes and never meant to hurt, gain favor nor riches from another.

"Joe was good-natured and he saved his cussin' and drinkin' for special occasions and in appropriate doses.

"Joe was humble and proud, but never prideful or boastful.

Old Joe

"Joe made sound decisions, had a clean conscience, was kind and trustworthy.

"About the meanest thing he ever said to someone was, 'you 'ought'ta have your ass kicked.' But we all know that more than likely, it was a justifiable comment based upon Joe's personal observation of a situation.

"Joe was well respected and as good 'a ranch hand as they come.

"He was never too concerned with fancy store-bought flneries and was completely satisfied with owning mostly necessities. He said it was easier to keep track of a few things than a whole buggy load of stuff.

"The things Joe owned were precious to him. He took good care of everything and felt blessed to have the simplest of tack and supplies.

"He always rode good horses, and his favorites were all foals of Little Lassie.

"Joe loved a beautiful red-haired Irish woman, made a promise to her one precious beautiful day near the edge of a creek, and kept it whole-heartily every day of his life.

"Joe dedicated his life and everything he did to those he loved. I doubt that many people heard the words, 'I love you' from his lips... but we didn't have to hear it... we all lived it... and felt it...every day."

After taking a brief moment to collect his own wavering emotions, the preacher motioned to Matt, J.J. and Billy Joe. The three men moved forward to the casket and working together raised the cover.

There beside Joe's body was his box he had had from his childhood, complete with the random items he had collected.

Matt retrieved the box and handed it to Josie's companion, and the boys resumed their positions with their families.

Josie took the box and opened it up carefully. Ceremoniously, she paraded to Katie and presented the open box to her.

Katie looked into the box. She reached into the open container and retrieved the small delicate stack of letters bound by the faded red satin ribbon.

Holding the precious documents gingerly, she hugged them to her heart, kissed the package and returned it to the box. She then drew out the small scrap of blanket, held it out for display to the others and clutching it with both hands, moved back away.

Matt was presented with the open vessel next. He immediately reached for the letters as well, tapped them three times upon his chest, looked longingly at them and returned them to the box where upon he recovered the dried-up crusty leather pigs' ear. He looked at the peculiar treasure and gave half a smile to himself. After showing it to Katie and the others he returned to Katie's side.

J.J.'s turn was next, likewise he salvaged the stack of letters from their enclosure. Looking towards the heavens, he touched them to his cheek, raised them high above his head as though he was displaying them to an angel hovering above, then grandly replaced them into the chest and claimed for himself the small ball of dirty wool.

Billy Joe, following suit, took hold the the papers and paused. He began to move away with the letters, but on second thought, shaking them in the air, Billy returned them to their holder, choosing the tiny bundle of corn seed for his reward.

Josie sidled back over to her husband who took the box from her and presented it, lid still agape, for her withdrawal. Josie looked deeply into the box; tears were streaming down her cheeks. She wiped them away with the back of her hand.

Reaching into the treasure chest, she put her hand upon the written tokens of love, pulling them from the box, she delicately caressed the ribbon streamers with her finger. After a moment of reflection, she gently pressed them to her lips, held them there momentarily and then moving them aside, chose for herself the horseshoe nail.

She solemnly closed the box and walked back to J.J., handed it to him, and returned to the side of her loved one.

J.J. looked at the box briefly then handed it to Katie, who passed it to Matt; and once again it was passed to Billy Joe.

Billy Joe pressed his lips together tightly and shook his head "no" as he returned it to Josie.

Taking the box from Josie, her husband asked, "How about we just keep this here at the ranch for now?" They all nodded in agreement.

The friends, acquaintances and onlookers watched reverently. Some of them were left to wonder about the significance of the box and its contents. Others knew the full story by personal witness or by testimony of those in attendance of Joe's night of storytelling.

Many of the seasoned tough cowboys, who had been present the night of Joe's storytelling, fought back tears.

Remembering his calling as Minister, Josie's husband returned to the duties at hand.

THE TRIBUTES

"Katie," he asked, "Are you ready?"

Katie moved to the head of the casket and looking down at Joe placed her hand on the edge of the pine box to steady herself. What started out as a crackly, choked-up whimper soon evolved into an angelic rendition of a familiar melody…

"Amazing grace, how sweet the sound
That saved a wretch like me
I once was lost, but now I'm found
Was blind, but now I see."

The audience, at least those who could, spontaneously joined in with Katie on the final verse.

Following Katie's song, Josie took her place near the casket and recited…

"The Lord is my shepard: I shall not want.

He maketh me to lie down in green pastures: he leadeth me beside the still waters.

He restoreth my soul; he leadeth me in the paths of righteousness for his name's sake.

Yea, though I walk through the valley of the shadow of death, I will fear no evil; for thou art with me; thy rod and thy staff they comfort me.

Thou preparest a table before me in the presence of mine enemies; thou anointest my head with oil; my cup runneth over.

Surely goodness and mercy shall follow me all the days of my life; and I will dwell in the house of the LORD for ever,

AMEN"

Matt, Katie, Billy Joe, J.J., 12 sad children, 27 cowhands, and a dozen towns folk joined in with the Preacher and humbly repeated a somber, "AMEN"

Following the song and the recitation, and prompted by the Preacher, Josie and the others retreated back a bit from the casket to allow the other mourners an opportunity to say their goodbyes.

The onlookers filed past Joe one by one, patting the box with their hand, sniffling back tears, or somberly giving a respectful nod of the head.

When the funeral-goers had resumed their secondary positions around the burial spot, once again, arm in arm, the five returned to the side of their loved one.

Unnoticed by the crowd. discreetly placed near the foot of the casket was a small satchel. Matt broke away from the others and was first to approach the package. He slowly untied the cotton strings confining its contents.

From the bag Matt seized a leather cross made of fine lightly tanned calf hide. It was hand tooled with roses, a trinity knot, and a Celtic Tree of Life. The edges were expertly trimmed in an intricately braided stitch pattern.

Matt placed the cross next to Joe and speaking out loud remarked, "Thanks… Thanks old man…Thanks for life… And thank her too. Thanks for the Grand Adventure"

Matt turned to Katie. She wavered hesitantly as she fondled the Cameo she wore around her neck.

In due course, she acquired the sack and searched through it until she came across a white cotton handkerchief embroidered with a delicate rendition of wildflowers and a lacy tatted edge.

JoAnn Nyman

Setting it within the casket near Joe's folded hands Katie spoke," I know it's not your style, but maybe you can give it to your sweetheart." as she reached up and caressed the cameo once more. "We will miss you… We love you."

Billy Joe was next to obtain the bag and from it, withdrew a zebra jasper heart shaped rock and placed it upon the pillow beside Joe. "Take this back to the Angel who left it for me years ago. Tell her I don't need it anymore. There is plenty of beauty in my life everywhere I look."

Billy looked at Ellen Rose, his cherished children and the others, then to the trees and meadow nearby and lastly to the little creek babbling along its way.

J.J. attained the sack next and found within it the article he had added. There was a bit of a smile on his face as he held the green paisley bandana bundle.

The inner circle of loved ones knew it contained a biscuit, with a thin smear of freshly churned butter and a dollop of choke cherry jelly.

As he tucked the bundle into the casket J.J. explained, "Good Luck Old Man, give her a hug for me and share your treat with her. You might need a lucky bandana where you're going, but I know I don't need it anymore 'cuz I'm lucky enough to have had you in my life."

At last the sack was passed to Josie. From its confines she retrieved a page of fine linen paper rolled up into a scroll. Within the roll a sonnet revealed Josie's deepest feelings of love and gratitude for Joe and Mary Kate. It was tied with a bow of braided grey and black horsehair.

"Tiny Lassie donated the hair from her tail and mane for the ribbon." Josie stated as a matter of fact, "She'll miss you too. Don't worry, I'll take good care of her and that foal we're expecting in the spring."

After a pause and a sniff or two, Josie concluded, "I wrote you a poem, you can read it to her later." she said, "Until we meet again...God Speed."

THE FINAL GIFT

Josie's husband waited for a considerable amount of time before breaking the silence.

"I believe there is one more item to add to the casket before we close the cover."

He opened the Bible in his hands and there within the folds of the pages he produced a richly decorated certificate with beautiful calligraphy writing upon it.

It was folded precisely in half and then in thirds. He handed it to Josie who opened the document and read...

"May the road rise up to meet you.

May the wind be always at your back.

May the sun shine warm upon your face,

The rains fall soft upon your fields.

And until we meet again,

May God hold you in the palm of his hand."

JoAnn Nyman

It was addressed "To our Loving Father and

Beloved Mother"

and bore 5 signatures.

Kathryn Josephine   (Katie)

William Joseph   (Billy Joe)

Mathew Joseph   (Matt)

Joseph John   (J.J.)

Mary Josephine   (Josie)

JOE'S EPILOGUE

Well, that's the story of Old Joe.

A common man, fair, honest, mostly average in height and weight. The kind of man that could blend into a crowd.

A good-natured storyteller with a few grey hairs and scruffy day-old whiskers.

Not a hero or special in any way by worldly acclaim, but a mentor and example to all who knew him.

A man who never aspired to be wealthy, achieve high academia, political power or fame.

A man who never owned more than a good pack horse could carry.

A man who believed that biological genetics has very little to do with who you call family.

A man whose favorite poker hand was always a "full house".

A man with a strange nightly ritual.

A man who took a chance. A chance that changed his life and the lives of others.

A man who loved and was loved by many.

Old Joe

A man who treasured a green eyed, auburn haired young Las, and kept his promise to her until his dying day.

A man who dedicated his life to her memory and devoted his every action to others.

A man of **"Intrinsic Value"** to those he loved and worked with.

Especially...

Five Orphans...

whom proudly claimed him

as their Father.

Dedication

To my children John, Keri, Matt, Joshua, Katie and MacKenzie who unknowingly allowed me to use their names and characteristics within these pages.

To Josie, the child we never had.

To the Joseph and Mary Kates in my life who have taught me so much about things of importance in this earthly existence.

And last but not least to my sweetheart John for his patience, unconditional love, support and holding down the ranch through all the hours I spent on this

and all my other

"Grand Adventures",

the wonderful man in my life who embodies the same

charitable spirit as "Joe".

As Joe would say, simply and to the point…

"Thank you."

JoAnn Nyman

Old Joe

ABOUT THE AUTHOR

JoAnn Nyman lives in North Logan, Utah with her husband.

She is the mother of a blended family of 6 children, grandmother of 20,

and great grandmother of 3.